BETWEEN THE *shadows*

A Shadows of Synd Novella

E. ABRAHAM

DEDICATION

For those who love emotional damage.

To everyone who doesn't—
I'm sorry.
I truly am.

AUTHOR'S NOTE

Between the Shadows is a Shadows of Synd novella. It is intended to be read after Under the Shadows, but can be read later on in the series as well. It centers around the relationship between Samantha and the Kings. Certain events within the novella have happened further along within the series and therefore might be minor spoilers.

Content Warnings:
Sexually Explicit Scenes (including multiple partners)
Adult Language
Light BDSM

One

Sam

"Wakey, wakey," Alex murmurs in my ear.

Stretching my arms above my head, I yawn, then snuggle closer to Alex's strong, warm body. His hand ghosts down my side and a shiver runs through me.

I'm still not used to waking up every morning within their arms. I keep waiting for the day I'll open my eyes and I'm back in my old bedroom, Mason still in the hospital, the Kings still refusing to help me, and the Guild still terrorizing Synd. Every day I don't, my heart heals a little more.

"Seriously, you two are still in bed? It's almost ten," Shane says, shutting the bedroom door behind him.

He stalks across the room and into the closet. I roll over, squishing my face into Alex's chest, and his arms wrap around me. Shane digs through the drawers making a racket, and I peek over the covers to spy on him. It's not often he comes busting into one of the other's rooms when I'm in their beds.

"Think we can get him to join us?" Alex's voice holds a tinge of laughter before he drops a kiss on the top of my head.

"I think he's a little preoccupied raiding your drawers. Plus, you know he likes to schedule group sexy time."

I brush my hand along his ribs, and he squeezes my ass. I push my leg between his, hoping Shane doesn't force us to get up. With nothing planned this weekend, what better way to start the day than a little fun with Alex? His hand slips under the band of my sleep shorts and he groans, eyes falling shut.

"Are you telling me you weren't wearing underwear the entire fucking night and I didn't notice?"

"Not my fault you crashed in the middle of a sentence. I was more than willing—"

"Stop talking or I'm not going to wait until Shane leaves before sinking into this pretty little pussy of yours," he growls, fingers digging into my flesh.

Alex dips his head, burying his face into my neck as he rolls me onto my back. Running my hands up his chest, I slide my fingers in his hair. It's long enough to yank on, and he slams his lips to mine, moaning into my mouth. Our tongues duel until he eases back, kissing me gently. More and more, he's been loving on me rather than ravishing me in the middle of the day. It's been slow and sensual—so different from what we had in the beginning, but I'm not complaining.

"Stop fucking and get up. We have shit to do today," Shane grumbles from next to the bed.

Alex pulls back to nip at my neck, and my eyes meet Shane's piercing blue ones. I grin and he scowls. I don't know why he's so insistent we get up. Lifting my hand, I wiggle my fingers, hoping to erase the terrible mood he's been in lately.

"I'm not wasting my time today, Princess. Some of us have shit to do, so get out of the fucking bed."

Alex's head whips up as the grin slides from my face. It's been a while since Shane's words cut into me like a dagger stabbing into my soul. I forgot how much it hurts.

He's been short with everyone lately. Clearly, something is going on with him, but he's not talking to me. I've tried to get him to open up. Every time I do, he tells me to leave it be. It hurts to be constantly shut out. It feels like we're right back where we started, and I can't help but wonder if his feelings have changed along with his attitude.

My stomach tightens as doubt swirls through my body. I push at Alex, and he glances down, concern lining his green eyes. I shake my head, nudging him again. Sighing, he rolls clear off the bed and stomps to the bathroom, bare feet slapping against the hardwood floors.

At the threshold, he turns back, jabbing a finger in Shane's direction. "You're an asshole. Spending time with Sam, regardless of what we're doing, is not a waste. And you saying that shit is fucked up. We've all been walking on goddamn eggshells around you for the last month and we put up with it, but you're taking shit too far now. Figure your shit out or I'll figure it out for you."

I jump as he slams the bathroom door, and hold my breath to keep the tears at bay. I launch myself away from Shane and roll out of the bed. Alex's black hoodie at my feet is exactly what I need. I snatch it up and pull it over my head. Hiding within the hood, I finally spin back to face Shane, still frozen where I left him.

"Is that true?" he murmurs, staring at his palms.

"Is what true?"

"You thought I meant you're a waste of time? That everyone's been tiptoeing around me?"

His eyes meet mine from across the room. I don't know how to respond. Alex was right, but Shane looks so devastated, I can't pile more on him. He's clearly going through something, and if it's the process of letting me go, there's nothing I can do about it.

When he first started snapping at me, I got pissed and snapped back. The longer he brushes me off, the more apathetic I become. It still hurts when he catches me off guard, but if I see it coming, I can protect my heart from the pain.

"You're stressed. There's a lot going on. Don't worry about it. Alex will get over it," I say, tucking my trembling fingers into the front pocket.

He drops his hands, and they hang loosely by his sides. "Will you?"

"What am I supposed to be getting over, exactly?"

Shane crosses his arms and tucks his chin to his chest. I brace myself for what I already know he'll say. Denial swirls in me as the taste of rejection hits my tongue. I open my mouth to delay the inevitable, but snap it shut when the door next to me opens and Ren waltzes in. He freezes when he takes us in, and I use the opportunity to make my escape. As I slide past him, Ren snatches my arm.

"What's wrong?" he mutters, tipping his head down. His dark hair falls over his forehead.

"Nothing. I'm hungry. Come find me when you're done?"

I plaster on a bright smile I'm sure he can see through, and he nods, squeezing my arm before dropping it. Shane calls my name as I slip out the door, but I pretend not to hear.

My stomach knots as I march toward the kitchen. I'm sure I'd throw up whatever I ate. It's not often I lie to them, and I'm sure Ren could tell I wasn't going to eat. I wasn't about to admit I needed to run. It's been a long time since the desire to flee has overwhelmed me. My palms itch and I swear my leg is twitching, even though I'm walking.

"Sam?" Emma's voice floats from behind me, and I glance over my shoulder, spying her tear-filled face poking from a random bedroom.

I shoo her inside as I pivot around and hustle toward her. Shutting the door behind me, I lean against the wood. I'm pretty sure I heard yelling as I passed Alex's bedroom, but I refuse to be pulled into that. Ren and Alex will want me to cuss Shane out—stand up for myself. Shane will be stoic and refuse to say anything. And I'll be stuck, wishing I could be anywhere but in the middle.

If Shane wants me to leave, he's going to have to tell me himself. No more beating around the bush and taking his shitty attitude out on everyone else. I won't fight him on it. I can't stick around if he doesn't want me, even if that means leaving Ren and Alex. I shudder, thinking about finding somewhere else to live.

But if he doesn't love me... The thought barrels into me, knocking the breath from my lungs.

Months have passed since I've felt insecure in my relationships with each of them. The peace of being with them healed the loneliness I didn't even realize had engulfed me. My life didn't have purpose before them. At least, not in the way I wanted. I wanted more, and I found it with them. They make the parts of my life I enjoyed before worthwhile, and the parts I didn't more manageable.

"Sam, are you okay?"

Emma's voice cuts through my panic and I straighten, forcing my face into the mask I rarely feel the need to put on anymore. Doing so makes my soul feel empty—lifeless. But as a teenager, Emma doesn't need the extra burden of my relationships with the men raising her. Besides, she's clearly upset, and her problems trump my own.

"I'm fine. What's wrong?" I ask, pushing off the door.

"You're not, but I know you won't tell me what's going on," she says bitterly, puffs of dust floating up as she sinks onto the bare mattress.

No one uses this bedroom, and the scarce furniture has a layer of dust on it. The only evidence of someone being here is the single white flower in full bloom resting in a vase by the window. I make a mental note to tell someone to clean the space, then shake my head. I might not be here long enough to pack, much less direct the cleaners to widen their scope of work.

"Don't be like that. Tell me what's going on and who I need to stab."

I grin, but she doesn't return my smile, and I sober. Usually that line never fails to illicit at least a small chuckle from her, even if she does it out of pity.

"I told him," she whispers.

I heave out a sigh. I knew this moment was coming, but I didn't think it would happen anytime soon. Emma may have matured in the last couple years, but she still holds an edge of naivety, which I haven't tried to squash.

I wish I could have lived in the dark about the atrocities in our world much longer than I was allowed. I never had that chance, but I can give it to Emma. Mastering the balance between her training and still being a kid is a process she's slowly learning. No matter what safeguards we put in place, though, no one could have saved her from her first heartbreak.

Sinking next to her, I lace our fingers together while we stare at the door. "I'm guessing it didn't go like you thought it would?"

"I knew he'd say I was too young. I mean, I *know* I am. I'm not stupid," she mutters.

"No, you're not. And neither is he. So, why'd you say anything at all?"

"Because I couldn't live with this feeling inside me anymore," she cries, exploding up from the bed.

Tears fill her eyes as she waves her hands around, then she lets out a strangled cry, more frustration than anguish. She buries her face in her hands before running them through her hair. I wait as she settles next to me again, and I notice the trembling of her body.

"What'd he say, Emma?" I murmur, holding my hand out again, and she grips it tightly.

"He was so...mean. At first, he was trying to let me down easy. I told him I didn't want anything from him, I just needed him to know how I felt. I thought he'd just say I was too young and then we could go back to being friends," she says, and I can't hold back my groan. "Stupid. Yeah. But what else was I supposed to do? I told him we could just pretend I didn't say anything, and you know what he did?"

"I'm afraid to ask."

"He fucking laughed. What kind of asshole laughs when someone is crying in front of them? Someone who just spilled their heart out? It hurt, so I—"

She swallows hard, and I tense. There are only a few ways this could have gone, though I didn't think he'd be such a dick toward her. Emma's crush was just that—a crush. I was convinced she'd never say anything, at least until she was legally an adult. It's not like he'd make a move on her. Not with the age difference between them. He's always been respectful and clear, so I never worried, and I pushed the guys to do the same.

"What'd you do, Emma?"

"I may have yelled at him, which doesn't seem bad, but it was...I cussed him out. Told him he was a fucking bastard. Everything would have been fine if he just would have stuck to the plan." A sob catches in her throat.

"The plan in your head that he had no idea about?"

"Well, when you put it like that, it seems unreasonable," she grumbles, and I chuckle. She sobers and drops her head in her hands. "And the worst part? He said it wouldn't even matter if I was old enough. He said he was just putting up with me because of my brother. Said he'd be floated if he told Shane how he really felt. Apparently, I'm a bitch who's selfish and spoiled. He just wouldn't stop talking. It was like he'd bottled up every little thing he hated about me and just threw it back at me. I didn't even recognize him anymore. He was supposed to be my friend."

She dissolves into tears, crumpling in on herself, and I rub her back. There's nothing I can say that will make her feel better. From experience, it's something she has to ride out. Hopefully, she doesn't become jaded like I was.

I remember when Mason accused me of crushing on Colin—which, gross—but also, Colin knew better. He outed me to Mason, told him it was actually a prospect named Jimmy, and Mason freaked. My brother ran his mouth about it in front of a group of them, including my crush. The complete disgust on Jimmy's face was enough to swear me off boys for years, which was probably Mason's goal. I'm sure he didn't expect the crippling self-loathing that came with it, though.

"Listen, he shouldn't have been an asshole, and I can talk to Alex or Ren if you want him gone. I'm sure we can find somewhere to take him so you don't have to see him anymore. Would that help?" I ask gently.

"No. I won't use my connections to ruin his life. I'll just stay away from him. But maybe you can have him moved? Just for a little while. I don't think I can handle seeing him when I pass the guard shack on my way to school. It just hurts. Why does it hurt? Shouldn't I be mad?"

"You're feeling everything at once, which is normal. First crush. First heartache. First asshole. It morphs. Why don't you go take a shower and we can get some ice cream, hide away in the theater room, and binge watch something?" I try to infuse my tone with both sympathy and excitement, but when she glances at me, I realize I failed.

"Are we hiding away because of me or because my brothers are down the hall, screeching at each other, most likely because of you?" Her eyebrow pops up and I huff.

"I'd like to spend as much time with you as possible before you leave tomorrow, so maybe it's for both of us."

Her head tilts, processing my words. "Hiding won't fix anything. Don't move him. Keep him right where he is."

"Alright." Bounding up, I clap my hands together. "Now, how about that movie day?"

"I think I'm just going to take a shower and then nap. You should talk to Shane. Something's going on with him, and he won't say anything to me, so I'm assuming it's because he thinks I'm too young to know. But he'll open up to you. He trusts you."

She gives me a small smile, wrapping her arms around her waist before making her way out the door, leaving me alone in a barren room that matches the gaping hole where my hope resided. Crumpling on the floor, tears fill my eyes as I wonder if this was all just temporary, instead of my happily ever after.

Two

Sam

"You're not eating," Ren says, collapsing next to me at the kitchen table.

Pushing the pasta around my bowl, I stab a noodle and shove it in my mouth. "Eating," I mumble.

"I'm guessing you heard us yesterday?" he says as he starts in on his own pasta.

"Wasn't eavesdropping."

"Didn't say you were. They weren't exactly being quiet. And you've been avoiding us ever since. You even slept in your own room last night, which I'm pretty sure you've never done. So why don't you stop skirting around the issue and start talking?"

He continues eating, not even looking up, and relief floods me. This is one of the reasons I love Ren so much. He pushes, but doesn't put me on the spot unless it's in the bedroom. There he expects me to submit, but any other time, he assumes I can deal with my shit accordingly. He knows when I need to be pushed and when to back off.

"Emma and I had a sleepover last night. She needed a little girl time," I mumble.

Appreciating Ren's ability to read my emotions is one thing, but that doesn't mean I'm going to start confessing my issues with Shane. Besides, in the end, Ren won't be able to change anything. Shane's choices are his own and no matter how much Ren and Alex badger him, Shane will do whatever he wants. I'll lose not one relationship, but three—four if you include Emma. The city will dissolve into chaos, and we'll be right back where we started, leery and distrustful of those around us.

"That's not all, but if you're not ready to talk about it, fine. You should talk to Shane. Something is going on with him, and he needs someone to pull his head out of his ass for him. You're the best person to get him to open up."

He shovels another mouthful in as he pulls his phone from his pocket. This is the second time someone has told me I have some sort of power over Shane. My heart aches, knowing they're all wrong.

Despair crashes into me, and I push my bowl away. I don't even have the energy to take it to the sink, and the one noodle I ate turns in my stomach. I mumble some nonsense about forgetting something and stumble from the room, barely making it to the bathroom before I'm gagging. Tears stream down my face, and I give myself over to the emotions coursing through me.

I jolt at a knock on the door. Swiping the back of my hand across my mouth, I heave to my feet. I splash water on my face, then pat it dry, spying my reflection. I can't help the fact I look like I've been bawling or that all the color has drained from my face. Resigning myself to making up more excuses, I yank the door open and freeze as Shane's scowling face fills my vision.

"What the hell is wrong with you?" he grunts.

"I think the pasta is bad. I should tell Ren." I lean to the side to slide around him, but he blocks the way.

He huffs, averting his eyes, and runs a hand through his hair. He always pulls that move when he's frustrated. Lately he's done it every time I open my mouth.

"Come on. We need to talk." He marches away, but my feet refuse to move. Glancing over his shoulder, he shakes his head. He faces me again, and crosses his arms over his chest.

"I can't right now," I whisper, wondering if he'll let me get out of this conversation for one more day. I need to know the plans he has for me, but the terror coursing through me is enough to try to stall.

"This can't wait anymore. Let's go."

I bite the inside of my cheek and school my features into the familiar mask I put on at galas and parties—any time I'm in public, really. If I can cut off my emotions, maybe I'll get through this without breaking down.

My feet are slow at first, but as he starts walking again, I speed up, keeping just behind him. I feel like a child on their way to be scolded, but when faced with heartache, I'll hide as long as possible. At least I can't see his face this way.

I expect him to lead us to his bedroom, but he turns toward his office, and my heart skips a beat. Breaking up with me from behind a desk is exactly on form for him.

"Fucking asshole," I breathe, and he casts me a confused look over his shoulder, but doesn't slow.

Closing the door behind me, I shuffle to the window to lean against the sill, my mind flashing back to when I slipped through it over a year ago. My heart was pounding then much the same way it is now. I wouldn't admit it to myself, but I was enamored with the mafia leader. He was always such a mystery.

"You going to sit?" he asks, settling in one of the chairs facing his desk instead of behind it.

"Can we just get this over with?"

"The shit Alex said yesterday—" He clears his throat, and I peer out the window. "I didn't realize I was being so obvious."

"Not hard to figure out something is eating at you. You're not that great at hiding shit," I murmur, watching the shadows lengthen in the setting sun.

"Apparently I am, since none of you figured out what the fuck was wrong." He chuckles, as if this is some big joke.

"Oh, I know exactly what's wrong, so we don't even have to talk. I'm sure the other two will push back. You'll have to deal with that, which won't be great, but I'm sure they'll get over it. Might be pissed for a while, though."

A tear slips free, and I angle my face fully away from Shane. So much for keeping my emotions in check.

"I hardly think they'll be pissed."

Rage rushes through me, and I spin to face him. "You really think they won't fucking care? Just because you don't anymore? Fuck you, Shane King. Go to fucking hell."

I rush for the door, and he curses. Before I reach the handle, I'm lifted off my feet, Shane's arms tight around my middle. I kick out, but the fight bleeds from me as I break down. I wanted to be strong, but the empty hole in my chest eats away at my resolve. Shane's low voice murmurs in my ear, but the roaring in them drowns him out.

He spins and slides down, leaning against the door as he traps me sideways on his lap. Sucking in deep breaths, I struggle to control the sobs wracking my body as my heart threatens to beat from my chest. Shane's arms are both a vise and a comfort around me, but it only sends my brain into overdrive.

"Sam, stop. Sam, please, just breathe," Shane whispers over and over.

As his words filter through, my breathing slows, my muscles relax, and my heart calms. I should push away—refuse his comfort. He's the one who triggered this ache in my chest in the first place, he shouldn't be the one to soothe me. But I can't help tucking my head under his chin, letting the warmth from his body seep into mine.

"Just put me out of my misery."

"I don't know what you're talking about, Princess."

The nickname cuts through me. I can't talk about love, so I settle on obtuse words to force him to admit he's fallen out of love with me. "Admit you're no longer in this."

He sighs. "Is that what you've been thinking? Sam, you've got it all wrong. You are everything I never knew I wanted, and that hasn't changed. Before..."

Leaning back in his arms, I take in his pained expression. I have no idea where he's going with this. Relief overwhelms my senses, and a soft sob escapes me as he rests his forehead on mine.

"I've been having nightmares." He sighs as his eyes fall closed. "Reliving everything. I'm losing my fucking mind. I didn't mean to push you away, but whenever we're in the same room, all I can see is you, bloody and bruised."

"But I'm okay now. I'm right here—healthy and whole—because of you."

"I thought you were dead. I can't get the image out of my head of you lying there...dead."

"I didn't die, Shane. I never died," I whisper, sliding my hand up to cup his cheek.

He leans into my touch. "You could have. And the last thing we did was fight because I'm a fucking tyrant. You deserve better."

I cover his mouth with my hand, stopping the words he'll spew out next. I've been silently battling his self-doubt for months. Shane never thinks he's good enough, or doing enough, or helping enough. Trying to combat his inner demons sometimes feels like a full-time job.

"We're not going there. I'm just glad you're not kicking me out."

He smirks before gripping my wrist and pressing a kiss to my palm. I shiver as he runs his nose along my jaw, then nibbles on my earlobe. His breath ghosts past my ear, and I twist my wrist from his hold to graze my nails down his chest. A groan rumbles through him.

"This is your home, Sam. You're not allowed to leave. We wouldn't survive."

"Can't blame me for worrying. Not with how you've been acting," I mutter.

"Sam." He cups my face and waits until I meet his somber eyes. "I will always want you. I will always love you. That will never change."

"Would have been nice to hear that a month ago," I whisper, shuddering as his emotions rip through me.

"I thought we got past all this. For fuck's sake, Sam. I got my goddamn dick pierced for you. If that wasn't enough to show you how much you mean to me, I don't know what will."

He guides me from his lap and stands, gazing down at me. As I smirk from my kneeling position, he rolls his eyes and crosses his arms. His shirt stretches across his chest, and a bolt of pleasure runs through me. I run my hands up his thighs, hook my fingers in his waistband, and raise my eyebrow.

"Something you want, Princess?" he asks, mirroring my expression.

"I think I've forgotten what it looks like..." I lick my lips as I finger the button on his pants.

Desire floods my body, sending a shiver that settles between my legs as he goes for his belt. Licking my lips again, I tug on his waistband to pull him closer, and he stops. His nostrils flare as I gaze at him, waiting for him to continue. He cups my chin in his hand, searching my face before his eyes travel down my body and flames course through my veins.

He tips his chin toward me, hands falling to his sides. "You do it."

With trembling fingers, I undo his belt and button, then push the fabric down as he whips his shirt over his head. I drop my hands as he kicks his pants off, leaving only boxer briefs behind.

I can see the balls from his cock piercing through the strained fabric, and my mouth waters. As he reaches over my head, my eyes fall closed, but instead of him burying his fingers in my hair, the thud of the lock echoes through the silence. A giggle bubbles from me as he leans back, but he doesn't smile.

"What's so funny, Princess?" He raises his eyebrow as he palms himself through his underwear.

I sober, recognizing the mood he's in. Most of the time we're a crashing of need, coming together to ignite each other's deepest desires. Every so often, he's sensual and sweet, usually when I've had a bad day.

But sometimes, like now, he craves the control. When his need to dominate comes to play, I push back. I'd never do that with Ren. *His* need for control comes from an entirely different place.

"Just wondering when you got shy," I say, smirking.

Grabbing his underwear, I yank them down. A growl from deep in his chest rolls over me before his fingers dig into my hair. He twists the strands and forces my eyes to his. My gaze dips, and I take in the four rods marching from the base of his cock toward the tip. My lips part and I lean forward, huffing when he tugs my head away.

"Open up," he commands, his voice rough.

Rolling my eyes, I brace my hands on his thighs. "I was doing that, you know."

A delicious burning sensation races through my scalp as he grips the strands tighter. "You could have done things your way had you not been a brat. Now, you're going to let me fuck your mouth as punishment."

I flush, instinctively dropping my jaw. The tip slides between my lips, and then he shoves his cock to the back of my throat. I gag, tears filling my eyes, and he eases away before punching forward again as he tips his head back.

Another groan leaves him as he continues to thrust. I dig my nails into his skin, breathing heavily through my nose. The metal piercings clank against my teeth. Over and over, he pushes into my mouth, and I gag before he pulls out completely, panting.

"Fuck," he breathes, rubbing his thumb across my chin.

Pulling me to my feet, he cups my face again, brushing away the tears, then captures my lips with his. I let him consume me, the flames of desire pooling in my gut. Gripping his sides, I dig my nails into his skin and his hand slides into my hair again, wresting control as he angles my head and deepens the kiss.

He shoves me away, and my back knocks against the door. We stare at each other, both out of breath. He points to his desk, and my eyes follow. It's bare, none of the usual piles of paperwork or laptop sitting on top.

I meet his eyes again, he grins, and it hits me—he totally fucking planned this. All my lingering concerns float away in the wake of the image of him fucking me on top of his desk. As I scramble atop the wood, his low chuckle chases me. Plopping on my ass, I cross my ankles, and lean back on my hands.

"Look at you, being such a good girl," he murmurs, and a shudder runs through me. "Take them off."

He gestures to my clothes, and I glance down. I'm still wearing the hoodie I snatched from Alex's floor yesterday, and I whip it over my head. I undress quickly before crawling up again. Shane's eyes rove over my body, leaving flashes of heat in their wake. He crosses his arms over his chest again, and my gaze travels down until it reaches his cock, which twitches. I bite my lip.

"You want my cock, Princess? You're going to have to earn it."

THREE

Shane

Sam spreads her legs, kicking her feet gently, and I swallow hard. Her fiery nature gets me hard every time, intoxicating me on every level. We're a crashing of two souls, devouring each other at every turn. The fact she thought I was no longer in love with her breaks me. It's not often I feel the need to be in control, but the last month has been hell, and I need this.

As she slides one hand across her stomach, inching toward her weeping pussy, I grip myself to ease the pressure in my cock. I could walk over and slam into her right now, give her exactly what she's begging for, but I resist. I have plans, and I won't let her derail them.

"Stop," I grunt, then clear my throat.

Sam raises an eyebrow before slowly removing her hand. She reaches up to pinch her nipple, making her pussy clench. I stalk to her and lean into her body. She sighs as I reach behind her, but she runs a hand up my chest, tracing my tattoos. I capture her wrist, placing it back on the desk.

"No touching," I growl. She pouts and I nip at her bottom lip.

"You're in a mood."

"Apparently, you need a reminder of where you belong. In light of your recent fears, I'm going to show you exactly what you mean to me."

She huffs, leaning back and giving me a look. "And that includes denying me?"

I smirk. "That's your punishment for not coming to me when you first started having those thoughts."

As she rolls her eyes, I thrust a finger into her pussy, and she cries out. When I curl it inside, she shudders, rolling her hips. I yank open the top drawer and grab the toy I picked up last week. I've been waiting for the moment to use it, and I shudder when I imagine it deep inside her.

Tugging my finger from her, she cries out again, this time in frustration. When she moves to replace my fingers with her own, grumbling under her breath, I drop the toy and grab her hand. I can feel her eyes on me as I suck my finger into my mouth, her essence exploding across my taste buds, and I groan.

She trembles under my touch, but I step back, settling in the chair facing her before my resolve slips. Gripping my cock, I stroke myself before gesturing to the toy. She glances down.

"What the hell is this?"

"I believe it's called a vibrator, Princess. Surprised you don't know what it is."

"I know that, fucker. Why the hell do you have it?"

She flushes when she finally catches my smirk and then her eyes drop to where I'm touching myself, twisting at the tip and then back down.

"Pick it up, Sam. No coming until I say."

"You've got to be fucking kidding me," she whispers while she finds the button.

Buzzing fills the rooms as her wide eyes find mine. I focus on her pussy instead of her flushed face. Fucking her mouth was overwhelming on every level. She's dropped to her knees plenty of times since she came to live here, but it's rare she gives up complete control. I had to stop or I'd cum all over her face, and I wasn't ready for it to end. She'd whine about not coming for weeks, too.

Shaking my head to erase the image from my mind, I track her movements. Slowly, she moves the vibrator to her clit as she leans back on one hand. Her legs dangle over the front of my desk, and it hits me she'll never be comfortable in that position, much less be able to come.

I heave from my seat, and she gasps as my hands circle her waist. Her legs fold around me, trying to pull me closer, even with the toy between us. She whines when I set her higher on the desk, but it's still not enough.

"Turn," I command, and she unwraps her legs and swivels so she's lying across the wood.

Lowering her to her back, she props her feet on the desk, the vibrator still buzzing in her hand as her knees fall open. I drag the chair to the side so I have a better view.

"Perfect. Continue. Remember, Princess—no coming."

She picks her head up, glaring at me from between her legs, and I slide low in my seat, leaning my head against the back of the chair. As she mutters under her breath, I scoot the chair closer to the edge of the desk to trail my fingers along her inner thigh. She quivers and grabs the vibrator again, bringing it to her pussy.

Every muscle in her body tenses when she touches her clit. Her legs start to shake as she circles it, her gasps warring with the buzzing. I can't help myself, watching her bring herself closer to the edge is too much, and I stand to bury my tongue into her core. She cries out again, hips bucking, and I rest an arm over her waist while I devour her, the vibrations rolling through my face. I don't know if she can feel it through my tongue, but I lap up every delicious drop of her, anyway.

With her legs quivering, core clenching, I yank the toy away, pulling my face back as well, and she screams in frustration at the denial.

"I told you no coming, Sam. Imagine my surprise when you didn't want to listen," I say sarcastically as I stand.

She huffs, then lets out a guttural moan. I grip her hips, dragging her to the edge of the desk, and slam into her. Bringing the toy to her clit, I thrust once, and she shudders, pussy choking my cock, spasming with her release. A strangled sob leaves her when I roll my hips.

"Hold it. Keep it right there," I demand, and her hand flutters up, wrapping around the base of the vibrator to keep it in place.

I squeeze her hips, fingers digging into her skin, probably leaving bruises behind. Good. Then the others will know who made her scream last. Plunging into her pussy over and over, the desk scrapes across the floor, but I don't stop. I can't. I'm so close to falling over the edge into oblivion, and I grit my teeth.

She spasms around me again and I thrust harder. Reaching up, I roll her nipple between my fingers, and she screams my name, one orgasm flowing into another. I still don't stop. Leaning down, I wrap my hand around her throat and her eyes find mine, desire swimming in them.

"Again," I growl.

Her eyes roll back and her back arches. Sliding my hand under, I hold her up, and she clamps around me one last time. I detonate, roaring her name as I spill inside her. The vibrator drops to the desk, forgotten. I collapse, burying my face between her tits.

Blindly reaching around, I find the button and turn it off, our gasps filling the space. Pressing kisses to her damp skin, I shiver as she runs her fingers through my hair. When she clamps around my cock again, shuddering, I grunt. Sucking a nipple in my mouth, her fingers dig into my scalp, holding me there as she arches her back. I roll my hips, causing her to whimper.

I lap at her skin before resting my chin on her chest. "Still worried?"

"No, but I'm going to need constant reminders in the form of multiple orgasms," she breathes.

"I'm sure that can be arranged," I chuckle.

Every time I close my eyes, all I can picture is Sam spread out on my desk like my own personal feast. I've been reliving it since yesterday, falling into my own memories. Of course, I didn't get any work done either. At least the vision in my eyes is her in ecstasy instead of being tortured.

I've been meaning to have a conversation with Emma as well, but she's been avoiding me. I don't blame her. If I had the choice, I'd avoid me too.

"Did you tell her?" Alex's voice cuts through my thoughts, and I glance toward the patio where Sam is reading, bundled in a thick blanket.

The last month has been a shitshow. As soon as life slowed down, I started imagining losing Sam. Dreams plagued me night after night until I just stopped sleeping altogether. When Sam started avoiding me, it only compounded my anxiety. When Ren and Alex started in on me, I lashed out. None of this was any of their faults, but it was easier to take it out on them than face reality.

"It's fine," I mutter, pulling bread from the cupboard.

I'd rather not discuss what's been going on. The other two haven't had any issues, so why would I pile my own problems onto them? Sam and I will deal with it in our own way. It's probably not the healthiest way, but at least it's ours.

"You've got to be fucking kidding me. You realize she's going to think the worst, right? Your asshole ways are going to drive her away. Don't fuck this up and break up our family," Alex says bitterly. "You won't like what happens."

"Going to abandon me and run off with Sam?"

I fixate on my sandwich. I should just tell him we worked it out, but his attitude is pissing me off. If Sam left, I know they'd follow. Hell, I'd leave too, even if she was running from me.

He braces his hands on the other side of the island. "Don't push it, Shane. Wasn't before enough?"

His words only serve to trigger the low-grade panic that's been riding me for weeks. The knife I'm holding clatters across the counter as my hand goes numb. My chest seizes, and I lean over, trying to pull air into my lungs.

Alex curses, but his voice is muffled by the roaring in my ears. A high-pitched ringing takes over, and Alex's hand lands on my arm. I jerk away. Stumbling, I hit the wall, sliding until I reach the cool tiles and my eyes fall closed.

"Alex, stop. You're not helping." Sam's voice cuts through the haze.

Her warm body presses into mine as she crawls into my lap. Wrapping my arms around her, I skim my hands over her soft skin, and my chest eases. She's murmuring something into my neck, but I don't even try to make out the words. Her presence is enough to calm me.

After several minutes, the door shuts behind whoever else wandered in, hopefully leaving us alone. Or maybe it's Alex fleeing.

"What happened?" she whispers, and I sigh.

"Alex is an asshole." I bury my face in her hair, breathing in her rich seductive scent to settle my racing heart.

"Did you tell him?"

"Tell him what?"

She wiggles closer and I tighten my hold on her. "Okay, that's a no. You should. They'll understand. Do you want to talk about the nightmares?"

"Not particularly." The ache in my chest pulses just thinking about it, but I have to tell her. "You're gone in all of them. Why would I put that on them?"

"Because they might be struggling too," she murmurs.

"Doubt it." I pull in a deep breath, bracing myself. "I didn't mean to push you away."

"I know. It's okay," she murmurs.

"It's really not."

We sit like that as the sun slowly sets behind the tree line. Every so often there's a muffled shout or stomping feet echoing through the kitchen, but no one disturbs us.

"Is that the only reason you've been..."

"An asshole?" I huff out a laugh when she snorts. "No, it's not. Shit's been too quiet, which puts me on edge. I could handle that, but Emma isn't talking to me. I know there's shit going down with her, and she won't tell me anything. Then you started avoiding me, and I understand why, but it only compounded the issues."

"We're kind of a mess, aren't we?"

"Ours is the only mess I'll gladly choose. Every single time," I mutter, pressing a kiss to her head.

"You don't have to worry about Emma. She's dealing with her first heartache, but she'll get through it. We all do."

"It was that prick Titus, wasn't it?" Sam smacks my chest, and I capture her hand in mine.

"Stop it. He's in a weird situation. Just leave it. She'll get over it."

Sighing, I kiss her palm. My little sister may have grown, but she's still more naïve than she needs to be. I was so bent on protecting her from everything in our world, I was blind to the fact she's a part of it whether or not I want her to be. Learning to protect herself is a better path than the one I had. In a couple months, she'll travel back to the same mountain camp Sam did to learn more about keeping herself safe from the shadows.

"The break at Aunt Marge's will be good for her, then. Now I know why she asked Greggers to take her instead of *him*."

"Give her time. She'll be okay."

"I should float him," I mutter.

"You will do no such thing. Not only would you lose a perfectly good guard, but Emma would shoot you."

I chuckle. "No smothering me in my sleep?"

"That's kind of my thing. She doesn't have my subtle moves yet."

Unwinding her body from mine, she stands. My palms itch to pull her back in, if only to hold her just a little bit longer. Our time together never seems enough. Something always interrupts, pulling us away until we can crash back together. We need more.

Four

Alex

Busting through the door to the conference room, I stop short when I spot Ren posted up at the table. I wandered around for a while after Sam kicked me out of the kitchen, but now I just have a bunch of pent-up energy with no one to take it out on.

"What's wrong with you?" Ren asks, not bothering to look up from his computer.

A mess of paperwork and at least four tablets are spread around him, but it doesn't even take up a fraction of the table. Half the time, I don't even know what he's working on. Not that I care. He's got his role and I have mine. I'm just glad we never have to switch jobs. We'd both fail miserably.

"You going to stand there and stare at me or start talking?" he asks, pulling me from my thoughts.

"Nothing's wrong. Why are you in here?" I grumble, collapsing in a chair down the table from him.

"Office was too small. Thought you were going to eat?"

I sigh, pinching the bridge of my nose. "Shane was in the kitchen. Still hasn't talked to Sam, and when I called him on it, he freaked the fuck out. Started having a panic attack like Mac used to have."

Ren's head whips up and he narrows his eyes. As he pushes back from the table, I scoff and he stops, raising an eyebrow.

"Sit down. He's fine. Sam came in and took care of it. Don't know what the hell is going on between those two, but he definitely didn't tell her what's going on with him," I say, folding my arms over my chest.

"You seem upset by that. You realize their relationship is their own. You don't factor in."

He settles back in his chair, going back to work. I scowl, even though he's not paying attention. Rubbing at the ache that's developed in my chest, I pull out my phone. Ren sees everything in black and white. He thinks if we just pretend we lead separate relationships, then there won't be an overlap. He doesn't see how connected we all are. If one of us fails, the rest will crumble, slowly but surely.

My phone clatters across the table when I toss it down. Tapping a finger on the polished surface, I open my mouth as Ren scowls at his screen.

"You're not seeing the big picture, Ren. We might all love Sam differently—I mean, not differently..."

I let out a frustrated groan, burying my face in my hands. I can bullshit my way through conversations, but it's hard to find the words when my entire life hinges on whether I can say them right.

"We do love her differently. Not more or less than one another, but it certainly is different. The big picture, though—"

I snap my fingers, cutting him off. "Yes, the big picture. If Shane pushes her away and she leaves, we all suffer. If he breaks up our family..."

Ren sighs, closing his laptop before leaning back to stare at me. "I understand your concerns, Alex, but that's not going to happen. After all we've been through, are you going to let her walk away without a fight? Is Shane? I certainly wouldn't."

"He's pushing her away just like he did before," I say sullenly, crossing my arms again.

"Ah, and therein lies the problem. Let me guess, you brought that up when you were cussing him out?"

"Not exactly, but close enough."

I don't know what he's getting at, but that's not surprising. Ren talks in half-formed sentences, only revealing what he deems necessary. It's fucking annoying, but after so many years of knowing him, I doubt he'll change.

"Did you know Shane hasn't been sleeping for the past month?"

"That's impossible. The longest someone has gone without sleep is two-hundred and forty-six hours, but the side effects of not sleeping would kick in long before that. He'd literally pass out, his mind forcing him to sleep," I say.

"Why you know that is beyond me, but that's beside the point. He's been avoiding going to bed. Instead, he randomly falls asleep at his desk in the middle of the day. He's clearly having nightmares, which I think center on Sam and our experiences." I grin and he rolls his eyes. "Not those experiences. The ones we don't talk about."

I sober. "Yeah, okay. Still doesn't mean he gets to be an asshole to Sam."

"No, it certainly doesn't. But they need to work out their issues alone. She doesn't need you to fight her battles for her." He turns back to his computer.

"There's a lot of things she's capable of taking care of, but this one isn't—"

"I'm perfectly capable of dealing with shit myself, Alex. I thought you'd have learned that by now."

Sam's voice floats from the corner of the room. It's like she materialized out of thin air. My brain short-circuits until the false panel behind her clicks shut. Shaking my head, I catch sight of Shane, holding her hand, still pale, but at least he's not spiraling anymore. I didn't even notice him next to her. Sam drops his hand and bounds over, jumping in my lap, sending both of us spinning as I let out an "oof."

"Seriously? I'm not that heavy." She pouts and I capture her lips with mine.

Pulling back, she tucks her head under my chin. Shane rounds the table, casting glances at Sam, almost tripping over a chair, and I snort. He scowls as he sits next to Ren, peering over his shoulder. Ren purses his lips, but doesn't say anything, even though he hates when we do that.

"You're not heavy, but when you land on my liver, I'm going to have a reaction, Bug."

She plants her foot on the edge of the table and pushes, sending us twirling again, and I pick up my feet. We're supposed to be going out to dinner in a couple hours, but I'm drained. I'd rather just stay holed up with Sam, worshiping her body.

"Shane's got something planned, but he won't tell me what," she murmurs as the chair comes around, and she glances at Shane and Ren before kicking off again.

"What do you think it is?"

"Not sure, but he's excited about it." She lies across my lap, legs hanging off the arm as she smiles up at me.

Glancing at Shane, I chuckle. "Yeah, he's totally amped."

She smacks my chest, her laugh filling the hole in my chest. Skimming a hand under her shirt, I send goosebumps scattering across her soft skin. She shivers as a slow smirk overtakes her face. When I reach her tit, I squeeze, and she bites her lip. A low groan rumbles from her as I roll her nipple between my fingers.

"Would you two knock it off? We're trying to plan shit here," Shane barks.

"Shane," Sam warns, twisting as she sits up, and I latch onto her hips, keeping her on my lap.

"Princess, I've got shit to do and hearing you moaning over there isn't helping me concentrate. I love you, but get a fucking room," he says as Ren puffs out a laugh.

Sam leans against my chest, and I tuck my arms around her, running a hand across her stomach before dipping down between her legs. She spreads them wider so her knees fall to either side of mine. Walking my fingers down her inner thigh, I peek at the other two. They're still engrossed in whatever is on the screen in front of them, mumbling back and forth.

"Want to give them a show?" I murmur in her ear, and she shivers, nodding.

Bracing her hands on the arms of the chair, she lifts, and I hook my thumbs in her waistband, shimmying her pants and thong over her hips. My hoodie covers her body for the most part, the hem brushing her upper thighs. It rides up as she settles on my lap again. Easing her forward, I free my cock. She shivers as I yank her back, and she drapes her arm around my neck, bracing her feet on the edge of the table. This chair is possibly the worst one to fuck her in since it has wheels, but I'm sure before long I'll have her splayed out on the table instead.

"How long can you stay quiet, Bug? Will you crack when I touch you? Or when my cock is deep inside that pretty little pussy of yours? Maybe when you're coming all over me?"

She gasps, whimpering when I squeeze her tits and roll her nipples. Trailing a hand down her skin, I dip one finger between her folds.

"So fucking wet for me," I groan, burying my face in her neck while I continue stroking her.

"Always," she says breathlessly.

I push a finger inside her, and she clamps down, flushing as her nails dig into my thighs. When she lifts again, I pull from her to wrap my hand around my cock, helping her guide herself down on me. As her heat envelopes me, I grit my teeth. It's been too long since I've fucked her.

We've been pulled in separate directions, or someone interrupts us. I shudder as her pussy quivers around me, basking in the feeling of being inside her again. I try to roll my hips, but the arms of the chair are in my way. Picking her up to ride me isn't working either.

"Fuck, I can't take this," I grumble, pulling from her heat and setting her on her feet.

She spins to face me, glancing at the other two, and I grip her hips, hoisting her onto the table and pushing her down. Whipping my shirt off, I tuck it under her head, and she grins. The ledge Ren had installed under the table is already down and she plants her feet on it. As I line myself up, I slip the tip of my cock in her, and she whimpers again.

Glancing up, I bury myself deep inside her pussy as my eyes meet Shane's. Grinning, I lean down, wrapping my lips around her nipple and roll my hips.

"You've got to be fucking kidding me," Shane mumbles, his chair crashing to the ground when he stands.

"You said get a room. This happens to be *a* room," I murmur into her skin before nipping at the other bud.

"Alex, less talking. More fucking," Sam wheezes as she kicks her hips up, squeezing my cock.

"Yes, ma'am."

Grabbing her hips, I thrust into her, harder each time, and her knuckles turn white from gripping the table's edge. I'm so focused on her and the pleasure rolling through me, I don't notice Shane until he's standing next to me.

Ren comes around the table, then sits in the chair I vacated. He wheels it around as he takes out his cock, and I smirk. Ren and I enjoy our girl together some, but it's rare Shane joins in. Sam won't say anything, but I know she wishes he would more.

I slow until I'm grinding my cock into her, and she huffs, bracing herself on an elbow to glare at us. I grin, pulling out until only the tip remains before punching into her again, and her head drops back. Shane leans down, capturing her nipple in his mouth while his hand dips between her legs, circling her clit.

"Such a wanton woman, spread out for us to worship," Ren murmurs as he strokes himself. "How much can you handle today, pet?"

"Everything," she gasps, meeting my shallow thrusts as Shane keeps up the assault on her body.

Her flushed skin is a tapestry of pleasure painted across her body. Leaning down, I sink my teeth into the top of her tit, sucking on her flesh. Marking her is Ren's thing, but I can't help myself. I need to taste her, mark her, make her mine, so she'll be reminded every time she looks in the mirror who she belongs to. Possessiveness rolls through me, and I move to her neck, biting down again, the sounds falling from her lips pushing me onward.

"Shane, make her come," Ren commands. "She's close."

Shane's hand, trapped between Sam's body and mine, jerks before speeding up. I push onto my hands, giving him better access as I thrust into her. I'll never miss an opportunity to watch her sail over the edge into oblivion. Her entire body tightens, and pure pleasure splashes across her face as she explodes, lips falling open, and a shuddering sigh leaves her.

Sam latches onto Shane's wrist, writhing as he continues to press on her clit. As her body relaxes, she tugs his fingers away from her. He twists his hand to capture her own wrist and traps her arm above her head. I grit my teeth as her pussy pulses again.

"Alex, finish so Shane can have a turn. Our little pet deserves more orgasms, don't you think?"

Sam whimpers, eyes finding mine, and I smirk. "I think Bug is feeling a bit empty, aren't you?"

She nods, wiggling closer to the edge of the table as Shane shucks his pants off. Tilting her head, her eyes fixate on Ren, still stroking himself, and she licks her lips.

"You want me in your mouth, pet?" Ren purrs as he stands.

Her nod is all the encouragement he needs. Shane tugs her upright, and I wrap my arm around her. When I pull from her, she cries out in protest. Cupping her face, I slant my mouth over hers. Our tongues duel, fanning the flames inside me. Shane's hand drops to her shoulder, guiding her to her knees, and I follow.

Yanking my mouth from hers, I pant, threading my fingers through her hair and tugging to expose her throat. Shane's hand wraps around her neck, whispering in her ear.

Ren steps closer, growling, "Alex, fill her pussy. She's going to need something to clamp down on, aren't you, pet?"

She moans, and my eyes trail down her body. I guide my cock into her again as she gasps. Shane grunts next to me and leans forward, using the table to brace himself. Our eyes meet and I smirk while he nods. His gaze darts to Sam's face and her teeth find her lip as they face each other. I hold her steady as Shane slides his hand to her throat and uses his thumb to push her head to the side.

"Shane, how far have you gone?" I grunt.

"Not exactly the time for this conversation, Alex," Shane mutters as Ren pushes his cock into Sam's mouth.

Ren grunts, tipping his head back as he surges into her mouth, and she gags. I hold her head still as he pumps in and out over and over.

"Just wondering if you want to fill her up completely," I say, waiting until Sam starts quivering in my arms before I dip my head and capture a nipple in my mouth. It's torture to stay still as her pussy squeezes my cock in time with her racing heartbeat.

Ren's harsh breathing fills the room and Shane whispers in her ear before turning to me. Her pussy clenches and her nails dig into my biceps, leaving pinpricks of pain in their wake. I can't hold back anymore, and I thrust into her in time with Ren taking her mouth. Ren groans and Sam echoes him, and then he's spilling down her throat. Her pussy quivers around my cock.

"Swallow every fucking drop, Princess," Shane growls.

When Ren tugs himself from her mouth, she licks her lips, and a tear cascades down her face. Ren catches it with his thumb, brushing it away. Leaning her back, I try to embed my cock into her, but this angle isn't the best.

"Lie back, Sam, so Alex can make you come again," Ren says, helping her down.

Gripping her ankles, I hold her legs to my shoulders, using them to keep her still as I pound into her. The other two descend upon her body, fingers raking down her skin, leaving red lines in their wake.

Shane dips, kissing her savagely, and swallowing her moans. A familiar tingling appears in the base of my cock and my stomach tightens. Dropping my hand, I circle her clit as Ren sinks his teeth into the flesh right above her nipple.

"Be a good girl and make him come for you, Princess," Shane says before swallowing her whimper again.

She convulses around me, squeezing until I explode inside her, my own groan rumbling in my chest. I spasm with each pulse of her pussy, riding with her through the orgasm, reveling in the feeling of being with her.

Sam's legs fall from my shoulders as she gasps for breath, and Shane shoves my shoulder. I'm not ready to leave her, but she's still writhing underneath me. I pull from her as I shudder.

"You can take more, can't you, Sam?" Ren says against her neck, and he sinks his teeth into her again.

Leaning back, he admires the fresh mark he's left on her flesh, and I roll my eyes. I don't care, but the satisfaction he gets from it doesn't make sense to me.

'Cept you did the same thing not ten minutes ago. Shaking my head to get rid of the thought, I concentrate on Sam as I take Shane's place. He doesn't ease

into her like I did, of course. He embeds himself in one deep stroke as he holds her hips in a bruising grip.

Skimming my hands over her flushed skin while he burrows into her over and over, I spy the telltale signs of her edging closer to another orgasm. Ren is working her clit again, whispering dirty words into her skin. I'm pretty sure he calls her a whore, but even if he did, she likes it.

Her back arches and her hips match Shane's thrusts. I see the exact moment she crumbles from the pleasure, and I swoop down to share in her ecstasy. Shane grunts and she cries out.

I'm pushed back and Sam is yanked upward, and then Shane is standing, his cock bobbing in front of her. Scrambling to her knees, she almost collapses when Ren tucks his body behind, one hand on her throat, the other between her legs.

Shane shoves his cock in her mouth, moaning as she swallows. "Clean his cum from my cock, Princess."

She shudders, swallowing again. As her throat bobs, he spills inside her mouth. He pulls from her, then falls to his knees as Ren moves his arm to her waist, keeping her upright. Shane cups her face, kissing her lightly as her body trembles, utterly spent.

"Well, that turned out differently than I thought it would," I mutter, grinning as Ren scowls.

Sam laughs. "I've got no complaints."

FIVE

Ren

I slip into my office and the lights flicker to life when the door shuts behind me. Dropping into my chair, I sigh, resting my head back. Shane isn't the only one not getting enough sleep. While he's been avoiding his bed, I've been pulled from mine more often than not. Every time he ignores a call, they immediately call me. I don't know when they started skipping over Alex and beelining straight for me, but it's annoying. He's probably rerouting them on purpose. Asshole.

"You okay?" Sam's voice floats through the room, and I jolt upright, whipping my head around to find her.

She's tucked under the desk in the corner, a book spread open on her knees. Why she's hiding in my office is beyond me, but I find her here more often these days than before. I assume it's Shane's recent treatment of her.

"I'm fine," I mumble, gathering the papers and shoving them into a drawer. I'd rather not be the one to give away our plans for her.

"You wanna try that again?"

I scowl as I slam the drawer shut, almost upending a glass with a white flower languishing inside it. The bloom shivers as the water settles. I spin to face her, wondering who decided to brighten my office without my permission. Shadows cover half her face, and a shudder rolls through me. Clearing my throat, I avert my eyes, gritting my teeth to stop imagining her on her knees again.

"There are a hundred different places you could hide out in this house, Sam. Why my office?"

I'm starting to regret giving her the code. Shaking my head, I huff out a breathless laugh. I'd never deny her entry, even to the one place I have that's all my own. Sam is one of the few bright spots in my life. If she wants to hide out here, at least I know she's safe—that she *feels* safe here—with me.

"You're hiding something. I won't ask what, but let's not pretend, hmm?"

She unfolds from her spot and saunters toward me. Leaning down, she braces her hands on my chair, a playful smirk gracing her plump lips. I used to be better at keeping my feelings under wraps, especially around her. After so much time, though, I lost the ability to hide shit from her. She's too observant, using all her skills as the Wraith against me.

"Don't you have a job tonight? You should get ready for that." I groan as she runs her nose along my jaw. "You're playing with fire, Sam."

She giggles. "I think you like it when I play with you."

A growl rumbles in my chest, and I wrap my hand around her throat, forcing her to her knees. She sinks slowly, desire dripping from her eyes.

"Wrong, pet. I fucking love it."

She smirks and that's it for me. I drop to my knees, slamming my mouth onto hers. Forcing her lips apart, I delve my tongue into her, my hand slipping under her shirt. I rip my mouth away, a curse falling from me when I find bare skin.

"No bra? Tell me, Sam, are you wearing underwear? Or did you come in here hoping I would strip you down to find a little surprise?"

"A wet surprise maybe," she says, raising her eyebrow. "You going to take care of it?"

"You'd like that, wouldn't you? You'd love for me to force my cock into your mouth, to lay you on my desk and fuck you until you can't breathe, to put you on your hands and knees and make you take my cock like the dirty little whore you are."

"Wrong," she whispers, leaning in. "I'd fucking love it."

I groan again, the sound reverberating around the room. Ripping her shirt over her head, I yank her to her feet. The flesh on her hips is soft as I grip them, before stripping her pants and finding nothing underneath.

She steps from the fabric, and I drop to my knees, burying my face between her thighs. Small hands grip my shoulders, nails digging into my skin through my shirt. I sink my teeth above her pussy, and her knees give. I latch onto her hips, holding her upright. As I lean back, admiring the mark I've left on her flesh, a hum of pleasure pulses through me.

Standing, I pick her up to set her on my desk. It's just wide enough for her to fall back on her hands. As she reaches for my pants, I shove her back. She grins as I push the fabric past my hips, then yank her to the edge of the desk and bury my cock into her soaked pussy.

Our moans mingle, intertwining before embedding within us as deeply as I'm buried in her. The desk thuds against the wall as I pound into her. Sliding an arm behind her, I force her to arch her back, never slowing my pace.

When her head smacks against the wall, I ease up, but she glares at me.

"Don't you dare fucking stop," she snarls.

Smirking, I freeze, buried deep inside her pussy, and she slaps her hand against the desk, letting out a shriek.

"You're a fucking asshole," she says, thumping her head against the wall. She wiggles her hips, as if she'll somehow entice me to start moving.

"And you've forgotten how this works," I say, rolling my hips and making her pussy quiver.

"Enlighten me," she gasps.

"Oh, my little pet. You take my cock and I tell you what a good girl you've been."

I duck my head to hide my grin, but she catches me, smiling back. It hits me then how utterly intoxicating she is. Loosening my grip, I slide my arms around her body. I pull Sam tight against me as I bury my face in her neck. Breathing deeply, I revel in this moment. Her legs wind around my waist and I thrust slowly into her, building the heat between us gradually.

"Ren..." she breathes, sinking her teeth into my shoulder as she shudders.

"Come for me, Pet."

Her hand steals between our bodies, but I bat it away, replacing hers with my own. She whimpers, back arching as I rub her clit, and then she tumbles over the edge, ecstasy stamped across her face. Watching her come is something I'll never get over, the sight sending me into oblivion with her. I press her closer as she shakes in my hold. I'm not ready to let her go.

"I'll never be ready," I murmur into her skin.

"Ready for what?"

I hesitate, my eyes falling closed. I'll never be completely comfortable sharing my emotions, though it's been easier with Sam lately. Admitting to her the insecurities in my heart sends a bolt of fear through me. Blind panic swamps me every time I think of her leaving, and anxiety dogs me whenever she sneaks off to a job, leaving me to wonder if she'll ever come home.

"It's just us here, Ren. Tell me. Please," she says, resting her head against my chest.

I clear my throat and whisper, "I'll never be ready to let you go."

She sighs, laying a hand over my thundering heart. I wonder if she can feel its rapid pace under her palm.

"Good thing I have no intention of leaving then, huh?" Tipping her head back, she gazes into my eyes as she grins. But I don't return it, and she sobers.

"You might not have the option, love."

It's the closest I've ever come to revealing my deepest fears for her. Even imagining losing her has my chest tightening and my lungs seizing. Darkness licks at the corners of my vision and I curl into her body, using her softness to ground me to the present.

She says something as I dig my fingers into her flesh, but her voice is muffled. I barely feel myself pulling from her warmth before I crash to my knees, burying my head in my hands. The logical part of my brain understands I'm spiraling. I can't breathe, though. I can't pull myself from the void beckoning me closer.

A small hand wraps around my throat, squeezing, and my vision clears for a moment, revealing Sam's determined eyes. Her mouth moves, but I still can't hear her. Then the pressure on my throat is gone, and she shoves my head down until my face presses into her lap. The smell of sex invades my nostrils, and the muscles in my chest ease enough to pull in a small breath.

"I swear I will withhold all things sexual if you don't start fucking breathing, Ren. For fuck's sake, you're dramatic." Sam's exasperated voice filters through, a tinge of desperation in her tone.

I pull in another lungful, and she curls over me, pressing her lips to the back of my neck. My fingers find her flesh and I skim my hands over her skin. As my mind settles, my senses return slowly. I don't know how much time I've spent on the floor, but she continues running her fingers through my hair. After another minute, I graze my teeth over her thigh, and she shivers.

"Ren?" she whispers.

My answer is to pull her skin into my mouth as I rake my nails down her body. I settle my hands on her knees and I shove them apart. Lapping at her pussy, I groan when her wetness hits my tongue.

Her fingers tangle with my hair, nails scraping against my scalp. My hand finds her shoulder as I bury my face between her legs, and I shift her onto her back. Tucking my arms around her thighs, I lick up to her clit.

Is making her come on my face the best response to having a panic attack? Probably not, but it's the one I'm choosing. It's the one I'll pick every time. She centers me more than anything else in this world. Which is exactly why the thought of her dying is so devastating.

"Please, Ren," she begs.

Swirling my tongue around her clit, I peek at her, and her brown eyes meet mine. Desperation and desire melt together, pulling at the corner of her eyes as her lips part, heavy gasps filling the space between us. Grinning, I hum into her skin and her body trembles before her legs snap around my head, squeezing.

When I push a finger into her pussy, sucking on the sensitive bud at the same time, she spasms. I add another finger and then drag them out slowly. She squirms, her body begging me to speed up, and I can't deny her any longer.

Drawing her clit into my mouth, I pump my fingers faster, curling them when her pussy tightens around them. Her entire body tenses, a shudder rolling through her. I drag out her orgasm as long as possible before I pull my fingers free and crawl up her body.

Sam whimpers when my cock brushes against her still-pulsing core. I'm hard again, but I doubt she has the strength to keep going. I'm proven wrong when her legs latch around my waist and the tip of my cock slips into her.

"Don't stop," she moans, trying to force me deeper.

I stop resisting, slamming into her in one thrust, and her back arches, a hiss falling from her plump lips. I capture them with mine as I surge into her again and again until both of us are gasping for breath.

Every time I hit the deepest parts of her, my stomach brushes her clit, and her pussy seizes around me while she cries out. I swallow each sound, drinking them in, her ecstasy transformed into living form made just for me.

She flames around me, shuddering as her nails dig into my arms. This isn't an explosion of desire pulsing through her. It's a quiet rapture of passion lapping at the edges of our hearts, easing us into a tranquility we only find within each other. I hold her longer than I usually would, if only to bask in her love for as long as she'll let me.

Six

Sam

"Alex, this is ridiculous. Why the hell are we up this early?" I groan, shuffling my feet as he drags me out the door.

His newly refurbished car sits next to the fountain. He keeps saying it's a classic, but I don't have the heart to tell him it's ugly. Alex is fucking stubborn and won't admit he painted it the wrong color. I freeze when I hit the bottom stair, tugging my arm from his hold.

"What the fuck is *that* doing back?" I ask as Alex shoots me a confused look over his shoulder.

His peals of laughter bounce off the stones when he spots what I'm pointing at. I circle around the fountain until I can fully see the gold hippo residing half stuffed into the bushes covered in white flowers next to the mansion wall. Whoever dropped the statue off clearly got interrupted in their mission. The last I knew this thing was in Reaper territory, but it always seems to make its way back to us.

"Last night while you were gallivanting around being Wraithy, someone snuck this beauty in here. Shane keeps pushing Tiernan off on the others. It hurts his feelings," Alex says, stroking the nose.

"You fucking named it?"

"Of course I did. He's been traveling around to our houses like a lost puppy. He needs a home. I mean, not here in the bushes, but you know. We should find a good place for him, don't you think?" He turns puppy eyes to me, silently begging.

I hold up my hands, backing away slowly. "Take it up with Shane. Not my business."

"Oh, Bug. We both know he'll listen to you." Alex laughs as he tugs me toward the car.

I snort, letting him stuff me in the passenger's side. Thankfully, he started it before we got out here and it's toasty inside. Holding out my hands to the heater, I allow the warm air to flow over my chilled skin.

The last few days have been cold, with freezing rain pelting us. We keep getting alerts for potential snow, but I doubt it will happen. The last time it snowed I was five or six. I barely remember it beyond a few snapshots of memories that dance through my mind as I'm falling asleep. Ren mentioned something about sledding at the Byrns' estate, but he seems to be the only one who remembers that.

I peek out the window at the sky. "Do you think it'll snow?"

"Doubt it. So, where do you want to go?" he asks, easing the car around the fountain.

I rear back, whipping my head toward him. "I thought you had everything planned. You *said* you 'mapped the day out' and I didn't have to worry."

His cheeks flush red, even as he smirks. As we pass through the neighborhoods, the sun rises slowly, casting a soft glow over the houses. I watch as he swallows once, twice, before gripping the steering wheel tightly.

"I just wanted to make sure you have a say in where we eat. Fuck, Sam. This isn't some grand master plan to get you away from the house or something. It's just a date," he mutters.

"You're lying." I narrow my eyes, tracking his movements.

The idea that he thinks he can hide shit from me is ridiculous and slightly insulting. Crossing my arms, I slam back in the seat, determined to ignore him. I'm sure if I pushed enough, he'd fold like a fitted sheet—frustratingly and by the end the corners won't match up.

I huff out another breath, something between a laugh and a sigh. I can feel his eyes on me, but I'm determined not to acknowledge him. If I forced him to tell me the secrets he's keeping, he'd beat himself up over it. I trust him enough to know it's not something I actually *need* to know, but it's still annoying.

"Don't be like that, Bug. I just want to spend the day with you." His hand brushes my arm.

"Then you should have planned shit better. If you wanted me to make decisions, then say that," I grumble, turning to look out my window, not really seeing the houses flying by.

He sighs as he eases the car to a stop at a red light. "Sam, I get it. You're hangry, you're tired, and you don't want to be in charge of shit right now. I've got it covered, but if I take you to some fancy-ass breakfast place and you don't want to go there, I need to know."

"If you know I'm hungry and tired and over shit, then why take me to a place where I'd need to be a pretty little princess for whatever media shows up to stalk us that day?" I ask, raising an eyebrow at him.

His eyes widen as the light turns green. He whips his head from side to side, before swinging the car around, back the way we came. Horns blast in his wake, but he grins as he glances in the rearview mirror.

"Where the hell are we going now?"

"You're right, per usual. So, we're going to the best fucking breakfast place in town." He grins before swerving around a car going the speed of a snail.

Minutes later, we pull into a familiar dirt parking lot, and I squeal, bouncing in my seat. Alex chuckles as he pushes from the car, and I bound after him. Tucking me under his arm, he kisses my head.

"I've been dreaming about their bacon," I say as I cling to his waist.

"I'm glad I could make your dreams a reality."

Several hours later, after breakfast and shopping, Alex parks the car in a space next to a pond. Not just any pond, though, *the* pond. The one I've spent more time at recently than I did all the years I was growing up. I've badgered all the guys into coming with me.

Surprisingly, Shane is the one who usually feeds the ducks with me. He even orders actual duck feed. I don't know where he gets it, and I'm not about to bring it up in case he stops. Ren and I spend our time on the bench with me tucked in close to him. Alex, though, is always walking, bounding around while I trail behind him.

They may complain about coming with me, but once they're here, they enjoy themselves. Or maybe it's just because we're spending time together.

In the middle of December, though, there's nothing to do at the pond. It's too cold to sit on the bench and the ducks have long since flown for warmer climates. Usually it's devoid of life, people rushing between the shops a block away, bundled up against the wind. My mouth drops open when I see the place teeming with life.

"It froze?" I ask, gaping at the pond.

"Yup. Colder than it's been in decades and the whole thing froze over. Thick enough for us to—"

"Skate on," I whisper, watching as a couple glides past us.

Alex pops open the trunk and I wander back to him, eyes still fixated on the scene in front of me.

"Alex, this is amazing, but I'm not dressed for this. Plus, I've never been ice skating a day in my life," I say, stuttering to a stop when I finally turn to him and huff out a laugh. "So, you *did* have something planned, huh?"

He smirks. "Course I did."

He hands me a thick jacket and then soft gloves before wrapping a scarf around my neck and tugging up the hood of the coat. Gripping the edges of the fabric, he reels me in, kissing me softly, and I melt.

Our lives are busy enough these days, filled with deals and meetings and running shit behind the scenes. It's not often we get days like this. A lot of the time it feels like we have to steal our moments, saving them up to sustain us through the lean weeks. The last few days have been a whirlwind of reconnecting, especially with Shane.

"Ready, Bug?" he murmurs against my lips, then tugs me toward a bench, skates hanging over his shoulder.

"Did you buy skates just for this?"

Sitting down, I pull my shoes off, shivering when the cold wind hits my skin. Thick socks flop into my lap and I grin as I pull them on.

"Sure did."

When I reach for one of the skates, he drops to his knees in front of me and gathers my foot in his hand before sliding it on and lacing it up. I wouldn't know how to do it properly, anyway.

"You look pretty good on your knees," I say, biting my lip.

Running my fingers through his hair, I grip the strands and tug. His fingers slip from the laces as he sucks in a breath before peeking at me through his long lashes. I catch his smirk, but then he ducks his head to continue putting my skates on. When he finishes, he switches to his own, and I narrow my eyes at my feet.

"Are they supposed to be this tight?" I ask, swinging my feet back and forth. "And this heavy?"

"Yes and yes," he says, pulling on his own gloves.

I hum, glancing around at the other people coasting around on the ice. I'm not sure if I'll be able to do this. Considering the fact that sometimes I can't keep my feet under me and other times I can scale the side of a building, the odds really are fifty-fifty.

"What happens when we fall?" I murmur before smothering a laugh behind my gloved hand when a man in a long coat slips, arms waving around before he crashes on his ass.

Alex busts out laughing. "That happens. But I won't let you fall."

He pulls me up and I teeter, my ankles wanting to give out, but the leather encasing them keeps me upright. Alex chuckles as I cling to him, and he wraps an arm around my waist, squeezing my hip. I'm not entirely sure whether it's to keep me upright or have me close.

Lately, he's constantly pulling me in onto his lap, tucking his arms around me, and cuddling me close. I won't admit how much I like it. That would ruin my reputation. There aren't many situations where I'm allowed to be coddled. I have to be the aloof socialite or the invisible Wraith. Being soft and vulnerable doesn't fit anywhere else but with them, in the quiet of the Kings' home.

"You realize you've never done this either, so who's to say you're not going to fall and take me down with you?" I snap, wobbling to the edge of the pond.

I'm not pissed at him, but the nerves are making me snappy. He gives me a knowing look before gingerly stepping onto the ice. Keeping hold of his hands, I lean, eventually letting him go. I tilt, my center of gravity off, but I throw out my arms to steady myself. Alex laughs again, joy bouncing off the ice and reflecting in his eyes.

"If I take you out, I'll make sure to cushion your landing with my body."

He beckons to me and I inch forward. As soon as the blade hits the slick surface, my foot slides with it, almost forcing me into the splits, and I yelp. Alex grabs me, his own feet going in different directions, and he crashes to his knees. I'm able to twist my hand away before he takes me with him. When I finally get my other foot on the makeshift rink, I expect to fall on my ass too, but I'm able to balance.

Alex struggles to his feet, slipping again before finally making it upright. "Did you know the blades used to be made out of animal bones?"

"Of course you have some random fact about this adventure."

As we grin at each other, he grabs my hand. Shuffling around, I slide forward and before I know it, I'm tugging him after me. It's not as hard as I thought it would be, but Alex is wobbling along behind me. I won't be going above a slow shuffle anytime soon, though.

"You've done this before," Alex accuses, and I glance back.

"Nope, but I do have excellent balance. We used to have to stand on two rods above a tub of frigid water for as long as possible. If we fell before they called time, we had to start over, while wearing clothes that would freeze to our bodies." I don't think about my time in the mountains often, but lately it's popped into my mind more.

"How old?" Alex grunts, his hand clamping on my arm, almost taking both of us out.

"I dunno. Maybe fifteen? I'd been there a couple years at that point. They start with easier stuff when you're younger."

"How many times did you fall in?" His voice is tight, hand squeezing mine.

"Not that many," I lie.

He snorts, then curses as a kid whips past us, her cackle echoing in her wake. We skate across the ice, and I feel like I'm actually getting the hang of it, even with the other people zipping by us, their faces blurry. How they all know how to do this is beyond me. It hasn't snowed, much less been cold enough for the pond to freeze over in years, yet they're all acting like this is a yearly pastime for them.

After an hour, my legs are burning and I've fallen twice. Alex tips to the side once again, ending up on his ass, legs splayed in front of him. I giggle, but he scowls, and I realize it might be time to go home. The sun is low in the sky now and I'm freezing.

"Let's go home," I murmur as he makes it to his feet, wrapping his arms around me.

"Good, my bruises have bruises and I'm fucking freezing," he grumbles, tugging me toward the brown grass.

The heat blasts from the vents in the car, but I can't stop shivering. I swear my teeth are going to crack they're chattering so hard. Alex turns toward home, hunched over the steering wheel. We make it halfway there before he's pulling into a coffee shop.

"We're getting hot cocoa with marshmallows and whipped cream," he snarls, rubbing his hands together.

"Are you upset about that?" I laugh and he smiles.

"I'm still cold. Don't be mean," he says, leading me into the shop, the smell of ground beans permeating the air.

He orders, then leans against the counter as he pulls out his phone. He hasn't checked it all day, but now he's absorbed in whatever is on the screen, and I sigh. Wandering to the back, I take a seat, waiting to see how long it takes him to notice. After five minutes, his name is called and he grabs the drinks. When he spins around, though, his brows pull low, glancing around the room until he spots me. A scowl overtakes his face as he prowls toward me.

"You wandered off."

"You were intensely staring at your phone," I grumble.

I shouldn't be upset. He's spent the whole day focused on me. There's probably a ton of shit he's putting off for this. I sigh again, cupping the mug and letting the warmth seep into my skin. I give him a sheepish smile and he leans over the table, kissing me softly.

"Sorry," I sigh against his lips.

Settling back in his seat, he gulps down his drink with a pained expression on his face. Clearly, it's still too hot to guzzle. I sip the chocolately goodness, licking the whipped cream from my lips. When I glance up, I find his gaze fixed on my mouth. I do it again, just to watch the desire build in his eyes. He checks his phone again, scowling as he shakes his head.

"Bug, we don't have enough time for me to take you in the bathroom and fuck you, so you're going to have to knock it off," he growls, his words sending a spark of warmth down my body to settle between my legs.

Squeezing my thighs together, I swallow hard. "Do we *have* to rush back?"

"Fuck," he breathes, ducking his head. "Drink your cocoa, Sam."

SEVEN

Sam

Twenty minutes later, we're speeding down the road, but as we pull onto the Kings' street, Alex slowly pulls off to the side. I raise an eyebrow, but he ignores me, grabbing his phone again. He's been checking it every thirty seconds, even while he's driving. I tried to ask what was happening, but he's ignoring my questions. Pursing my lips, I cross my arms. He taps his phone against the steering wheel, and I huff.

"Would you just tell me what the fuck is going on? What the hell are you guys hiding from me?" I snap, glancing out the window so he won't see the tears in my eyes. I don't even know why I'm getting emotional about this.

"Why would you think we're hiding shit from you?" he mutters.

He's distracted. I can hear it in his voice. He probably didn't even fully hear what I asked. Clearly, he has no idea how affected I am, which only makes me feel worse. A single tear escapes, and I catch it with my tongue as it slips past the corner of my lip.

"You want a list? Fine. Shane and I had all those issues, which we talked about, but now he's avoiding me again. Ren slams his computer every time I walk into the room. Plus, he keeps trying to distract me with his dick, as if I won't notice. And then you randomly want to spend the day together, but the end of it rolls around and you're ignoring me. Like you're doing right now!"

He's not even looking at me, eyes fixed on his screen. He whips his head up when I let out a frustrated cry. Reaching for the handle, I yank at the metal, but it doesn't budge. There's no lock on the door, so I slam my hand down on the center console to unlock it, only to be met with Alex's hand blocking my way. He wraps his hand around my fingers, stopping me.

"Sam, stop. I...I can't tell you what's going on, but if you give me like two minutes you'll understand. I swear."

Meeting Alex's pleading eyes, I pull in a deep breath, settling the nerves dancing in my chest. I start counting silently, staring at him the entire time. He holds my gaze, but I can tell he's resisting the urge to glance at his phone again. I never thought I'd be so pissed off at a piece of technology. The urge to rip it from his hand and toss it out the window is like a wild beast inside me, raging to be freed. I pull in another calming breath, willing the impulse away.

"One hundred twenty. Time's up," I growl, and he slowly releases my wrist as his phone vibrates.

He drops it in the cup holder and puts the car in drive, rolling down the street. He keeps peeking at me, as if I'll jump from the car if he doesn't keep an eye on me.

I just want a shower and bed. I'm sore from skating and this whole encounter has soured the hot cocoa swimming in my stomach. Maybe I can sneak into the theater and watch a movie by myself. I doubt they'll leave me alone, though. I could slip out the tunnels and flit around the city, find some trouble to get into. That would burn away the nervous energy rushing through me.

As the road curves, the mansion comes into view and my mouth drops open. Strings of white lights are draped everywhere—between trees, around bushes, and lining the guard shack. The car bumps into the drive, circling the fountain, lights highlighting the mermaid who has tinsel hanging from her mouth where water usually spews. I burst out laughing, tears filling my eyes for a whole other reason now.

"Where? How? Why?" I stutter, trying to find the words as he parks. "What the hell is all this?"

"Do you like it?" he asks, lacing our fingers together.

Every window is wrapped in lights, and more lay over the hippo. The bulbs hanging off the awning above the front door twinkle, creating a halo around

Ren and Shane standing at the top of the stairs. Ren's half smirk is in place and Shane looks nervous as hell.

"This is amazing. A little over the top, but amazing," I whisper. "Are those candles in the windows?"

"Every single one. They're not real. We're not trying to burn the place down. Come on, before Shane shits his pants."

I'm still trying to see everything at once as Alex tugs me out of the car. Stumbling up the stairs, I fall into Shane's arms. It takes me a minute to realize he's trembling.

"It's cold. Shane?" Ren says, sweeping his hand out to usher us through the doors.

The staircase inside is wrapped in garland, complete with red berries tucked in between the leaves and lights circle the spindles. There's a fully decorated tree with ruby ornaments hanging from the branches, a ribbon crawling up the sides to a brightly lit star. Shane's hands fall on my shoulders, and he leans down, breath ghosting across my hair.

"Do you like it?"

"Like it?" I spin slowly, spying more decorations splashed across the walls. "This is...I love it. But what the hell?"

Ren snorts, grabbing my hand to pull me deeper into the house. The entire place looks like Christmas exploded inside of it. When we pass the wall of windows at the back, I catch sight of the trees lining the property. Each one of them has more lights.

When we reach the living room we usually hang out in, I almost run into the wall I'm so distracted by the gigantic evergreen covered in flowers I don't know the name of reaching up to the ten-foot ceiling. I can't imagine how they got it in here. Alex drapes his arms around me, hugging me from behind.

"Almost every room is decorated," he murmurs.

"Why?" I breathe, pulling from his hold to drift around the room, taking in all they've done while I was out with Alex.

"You deserve something special, especially right now," Shane says, nerves lacing his tone, and I turn back.

"The last time I had something like this was...never. I've never had anyone do this for me. Mason tried once, but we were kids. It wasn't exactly something our dad cared about."

"What'd he do?" Alex asks, tilting his head.

"One year, everyone in school was talking about all these amazing holiday plans they had, baking cookies, and decorating trees, and so many presents. I never had that, and I wanted it. I wanted to be a part of a tradition that wasn't about demanding loyalty in order to maintain control." Shane and Ren nod. I'm sure he had the same lesson drilled into him growing up.

I close my eyes, the memory unfolding in my mind, and I smile. "He got me a little tree, decorated with tiny lights and small ornaments. He even got me a present to put under it. I kept it all until Dad found the tree and burned it in front of me," I murmur, slowly opening my eyes. "But he never found the necklace Mason bought for me. I was always too scared to wear it, though. Pretty sure it's tucked in some secret hiding place I've forgotten now."

"At least you have the memories," Ren whispers, pressing a kiss to my cheek.

My eyes widen when I spy brightly wrapped gifts under the tree. I spin around, forcing my face into a mask. The boxes are probably empty, placed there for looks and nothing else. For a split second, I thought they'd bought presents for me, but I can't afford to let that idea to take root. I don't fuck around with devastation. Not my thing. Thanks.

Perching on the edge of the couch, I force my muscles to relax. Ren sits next to me, ducking his head into my neck.

"What's wrong?" he says quietly.

"Nothing, this is great. You guys did so much work and I can't tell you how much it means to me." Tears fill my eyes again and I rest my head against his hard shoulder, a chill running through me.

"Liar," he says into my hair.

I lift my head and then jolt when one of the wrapped boxes lands in my lap. I raise an eyebrow at Shane, who smirks before stalking back to the tree. Alex hops over the back of the couch, bouncing next to me.

"Couldn't just walk around like a normal person, could you? Have to almost take her head off instead," Shane grumbles, setting another present down.

My mouth drops as he sets every single gift on my lap, then the coffee table in front of me when there's no more room. My heart might explode, it's beating so fast, overflowing with emotions I don't know how to process.

Gazing at each of their expectant faces, I don't know how to respond. The last five minutes have been a whirlwind of getting my hopes up and me smothering them, only for them to skyrocket once more. I don't even want to ask, but there's at least a dozen presents sitting in front of me.

"So, these three are mine?" I ask, lifting the three small boxes in my hands.

Alex bursts out laughing while Ren's quiet chuckle rolls through me.

"Princess, they're all for you. Start opening so we can use them," Shane says, smirking, and my breath catches.

Gingerly, I pick at the tape before Alex reaches over and rips a large section of paper off.

"Let her do it on her own, dickhead," Shane grunts, collapsing in a chair across from us.

"Rip it open, Bug. No one's going to judge you. This one's from me," Alex murmurs as his hand slides along my thigh, hand settling between my legs.

I squeeze my thighs together. He snorts, digging his fingers in, and I distract myself by ripping the paper off, revealing a nondescript black box. I lift the flap, the flames from the fireplace reflecting off the contents within, and I turn the box before giving him a look.

"Are these butt plugs?"

"His and hers." He grins, wiggling his eyebrows, handing me another present. "Open this one."

I tear off the paper, excitement bubbling up. "A cock ring? You've got to be kidding me. Does this thing light up?"

"Four different colors, and one of them is rainbow," he says, jumping to his feet and gyrating his hips.

Shane throws a pillow, hitting him square in the face, and I dissolve into laughter. Slowly, I make my way through the rest of the gifts. A cashmere scarf from Alex, a new knife sheath from Shane, and a smart watch from Ren. I'm pretty sure he's trying to track me, but he went on for twenty minutes about the features it has and how much it'll help me on my jobs.

A blush splashes across Shane's cheeks as I open an egg vibrator from him. "App-controlled" is splashed across the box and Ren snorts. He leans in, running his nose along my jaw.

"Don't worry, pet. I've already hacked it," he murmurs, and my stomach tightens.

"Are these ones from you?" I murmur, gathering the last few gifts to me.

"That they are." He leans back, lacing his hands behind his head.

A giggle escapes me when I find a box for a restraint system, complete with fuzzy cuffs. "I'm guessing the straps are already installed?"

He smirks before rubbing a hand across his mouth. Pulling the next box from the pile, I tear the paper away, revealing vibrating anal beads.

"I'm starting to notice a theme here. Did you guys plan this?"

"Not exactly. It just sort of happened that way. Last one, Princess," Shane says, handing me one more.

It's thinner than the rest, and when the wrapping is gone, I reveal a document envelope. Raising an eyebrow, my fingers tremble as I open the flap, pulling out a thin piece of paper. Confusion clouds my mind, the words on the page bleeding together. Deed is splashed across the top, but I still don't understand.

"Uh, thanks," I mumble, trying to stuff it back in the envelope. I really hope they didn't buy me a house.

Shane's hand grabs mine and our eyes meet. "Look again."

Skimming my eyes across the page, they catch on my own name printed under owners. I read it again, still not fully understanding.

"Did you...this isn't...Did you put my fucking name on the house?" I demand, the sheet fluttering to the ground.

"This is your home too, Sam. It seems appropriate we make it official," Ren murmurs.

Alex picks up the deed and holds it out to me. "Come on, Bug."

I glance at Shane, ever the holdout on these things. With everything happening lately, I wonder if he's still on board with something as drastic as putting my name on his house. In fact, I didn't even know Ren and Alex held a stake as well. Not that Shane would hold his fortune over anyone's head, but to put me on this is a huge step. He may be giving it to me now, but I'm so caught off guard, my mind is rebelling.

Shane holds out a pen. "Sign it, Sam."

I can't help it, I burst into tears. Shane snatches the paper away, and then their arms surround me as I sob into my hands. The fact I'm breaking down over this is ridiculous, but I can't stop.

After several minutes, I'm finally able to calm down. Shane hands me the pen again and with shaking hands, I sign it. I expect something to change, but honestly, I feel the same as I did before. My name on a piece of paper doesn't make this place feel any different. It was already home. Even after the shit with Shane, it always feels like home.

"Shit, I almost forgot," Alex yelps, running from the room.

"What'd he forget?" I ask as Shane sits next to me, pulling me into his lap and running his hand up and down my thigh as I tuck my freezing toes under Ren's leg.

"Don't worry about it," Shane mutters, sliding his hand behind my neck to pull me closer.

His fingers drift into my hair before he grips the strands and yanks my head back to scrape his teeth down the column of my throat. My stomach spasms along with my pussy. Ren's hand brushes my knee and I shudder.

"Spread your legs, pet," Ren says.

He tugs on my knee, easing them apart while Shane's mouth covers mine. The low flame burning inside me flares, engulfing me in desire. Ren's fingers graze my clit through my leggings.

Shane rips his mouth away, yanking my head back until my back arches over his arm. Heat floods me as Ren bites my thigh before sucking on my clit through my pants. In only one minute, they've riled me up so completely I'm ready to shatter in their arms.

Just as suddenly as they started, their hands and mouths are gone, leaving me bereft. I fall back on the couch, legs still splayed over Shane's lap. My pants are ripped from my body, leaving a delicious chill skittering across my skin.

"Arms up, Princess," Shane growls, tugging the hem of my shirt up and over my head.

"Move her," Ren says gruffly, adjusting himself when he stands.

Shane's arms slide under me before heading for the tree. They've clearly planned this, since there's a heap of blankets I didn't notice before piled under the twinkling lights. My body sinks into the fluffiness and I groan as my muscles relax.

My eyes track Ren as he grabs something from one of the boxes scattered about, then smirks when he finds my focus on him. Holding up the set of handcuffs, they swing from his fingers, black and fur lined.

"You don't want to tie me up with the lights?" I purr, fingering the string hanging above my head.

"I doubt that would be very comfortable for you. I'm also afraid you might break them. These though"—he murmurs, pulling out a bottle of lube, and I shiver—"will not only be comfortable, but keep you exactly where we want you."

Shane huffs out a laugh, leaning over my body to nip his way across my skin, leaving goosebumps in his wake.

"And they have a release for you, just in case," Shane rumbles into my flesh.

His mouth skims down before settling between my legs, and I kick my hips up. He slams an arm across my waist to hold me down. I try to wiggle closer, but it's no use. Finally, his tongue circles my clit before diving into my core and a cry leaves me. His movements are slow and torturous, stringing me along, and I close my eyes as pinpricks of light spark behind my lids.

Digging my fingers into the softness beneath me, I arch my back to get as much leverage as possible, but Shane continues his measured assault on my body. Ren's fingers encircle each wrist, guiding them above my head before the soft cuffs replace his hands. He latches onto the chain connecting them as he straddles me, pressing his naked body into mine. While Shane was distracting me, apparently Ren was shedding his clothes.

When I open my eyes, I find Ren's stormy eyes boring into mine. Glancing down, I find his cock inches from my mouth and my lips part, letting out a low moan.

"If you want something, pet, you're going to have to beg for it," he growls.

"Please, Ren?" I ask, then cry out, eyes slamming shut again, when Shane sucks my clit into his mouth.

Ren slides forward, shoving his cock between my lips, and I swallow, saltiness hitting my tongue. I hum as he gradually pulls out, then thrusts back in. I gag when he hits the back of my throat, and he eases back again before repeating the move. A strangled noise from the doorway has my eyes opening, revealing Alex staring from the doorway, a can of whipped cream in hand.

"Fuck me sideways, that's hot," he murmurs before the can clatters to the floor and rolls away.

As he stalks across the floor, he rips off his clothes. I track his movements until he's blocked by Ren's body. I cough once and Ren leans back, scooting down my body and pressing his lips to mine. Shane's mouth leaves my pussy, and a low whine comes from me unbidden.

As Ren sits up, I catch sight of Alex's sandy blond locks dipping between my legs and another moan leaves me as his tongue starts swirling around my clit. Ren takes full advantage of the distraction he's creating to push his cock into my mouth once more. I can't help but shudder as I watch his head tip back while he slides his cock in and out of my mouth. So many sensations bombard my body I can barely keep up.

"Ren, don't come down her throat. She needs to earn that shit," Shane growls from behind Alex, and I cough around Ren's cock.

I scrape my teeth lightly down his shaft as he pulls out, and he snarls at me. "You want to play games, pet? So be it. Alex, move."

Alex nips at my clit once more, and I jerk, my pussy clenching around nothing. Shane's hands replace Ren's on the cuffs, forcing my arms to stay above my head as Ren stands. Settling between my legs, he pulls one finger through my wetness before popping it in his mouth.

Alex crashes to his knees next to me, capturing a nipple between his teeth before Ren buries himself to the hilt inside me. My orgasm catches me out of nowhere, but I ride the wave of ecstasy as Shane covers my mouth with his, swallowing my moans. Ren thrusts into me, never slowing his pace as my pussy spasms around him.

"Should we use another one of your gifts, or would you prefer my cock in you as well?" Alex asks, then licks between my tits, a chill chasing his tongue.

I pull my mouth from Shane's as Ren stops, buried deep inside me, and I wiggle.

"Answer the question, Sam," Ren grits out.

"Cock. Give me your cock," I moan and then whimper at the sudden emptiness as Ren pulls from me.

Ren grabs the chain, tugging me upright, and Shane slips in behind me, his cock sliding between my cheeks. Alex shuffles me around to face Shane and then guides me down, straight onto Shane's cock. I shudder, but I'm not able to catch myself and my forearms land on his chest. He groans as my pussy quivers around him. I twist my wrists to stretch them when Ren frees one before he tugs them behind my back and replaces the cuff. I tip my head to the side so I can breathe.

Cool liquid spreads against my ass as Shane murmurs into my hair. I can't make out the words, but he's skimming his hands along my back. Then there's pressure and Alex moans as he eases into my ass.

"So fucking tight," he wheezes when he's fully seated.

Ren's voice rumbles through our harsh breaths. "Fuck her, Alex. Make her come."

Alex's hands wrap around the chain, using it as a handle as he starts to surge into me. With every thrust, Shane's cock twitches, creating a friction that causes me to spasm around him.

Alex grunts as he speeds up, and Shane's fingers dig into my hips, holding me still for his brother.

"Fuck her harder," Shane groans as needy noises fall from my lips.

And then I'm free-falling into weightlessness. Biting Shane's skin, I hiss as Alex follows me, yelling my name as he climaxes.

"Lean back, Alex," Shane says through gritted teeth.

Alex pants, hand rubbing my ass cheek. "Give me a fucking minute, for fuck's sake."

"Just lean back, fucker," Shane barks.

I can practically hear Alex rolling his eyes as he tugs the chain, forcing me to follow him as he leans back. Shane's hands grip my hips tighter, probably leaving bruises, and starts thrusting into me hard and fast. I'm at their mercy. Ren appears next to us, and he runs his teeth across my nipple, his hand sneaking down at the same time to circle my clit.

"Holy fuck, Bug, you're goddamn amazing," Alex says.

"Again, Sam. Make him come for you," Ren says before sinking his teeth into my neck, marking me as his.

Shane calls out my name as he erupts, sending another orgasm spinning through me. Panting through it, Alex rocks into me, and I thrash in his hold as I spasm around Shane's cock. I don't know how much more I can take. I'm already spent.

Alex eases me down before slipping from my body, leaving a burning sensation in his wake along with an emptiness. My arms ache from the position they're in and Ren releases them. They flop next to me, and Alex chuckles, running his hand up my spine.

"Did we wear you out, Bug? You going to have it in you to take care of Ren?"

I mumble nonsense into Shane's glistening skin, and he lifts me, cradling my body as he sits up.

"Where do you want her, Ren?" he asks, then presses kisses across my shoulder.

Bliss fills my pores, and I'm content for the first time in a long while. A peace settles over me as Shane positions my back to his chest, my legs falling over his, spreading me wide as Ren's eyes rake down my body. I quiver, sliding down a little more. Ren kneels, lining his cock up to my pussy, wet from both Shane and myself.

He drives into me, groaning as he does, and one falls from my lips too. Shane grips my hips, holding me still while Ren thrusts harder. Shane's hand wraps around my throat, forcing my head back and my eyes meet Alex's bright green ones as he sits in a chair, stroking himself.

"Do you like him fucking you while I play with your body?" Shane growls, as he walks his fingers down my body before pressing on my clit. "You like being our good little whore, don't you?"

When I jerk, he grips me tighter, then eases his hold on my throat. Ren groans as I seize around his cock. I barely register Ren moaning my name as he shatters, joining me in complete rapture. Shane lies back, bringing me with him, and Ren shudders as my pussy clings to him.

Alex walks over, still gripping his cock, and tilts his head as he gazes down at me sprawled across Shane with Ren still deep inside me. He grins, green eyes twinkling.

"Fuck I love you, Bug."

EIGHT

Final

Jerking upright, I blink rapidly, trying to dispel the shadows in my eyes. The darkness remains though, clouding my vision and filling my chest with a bolt of terror. I whip my head back and forth, pulling in steady breaths. Nothing changes and despair crashes into me again, overwhelming my senses.

A steady drip of water keeps time with my heart, echoing off the concrete walls surrounding me. I shiver as the constant cold seeps further into my aching body. A deep, cloying scent masked by decay invades my nostrils and my stomach turns.

I sway, almost tipping over when I unwind my arms from my legs. I've prided myself on keeping my tears at bay the entire time I've been locked away, but with the dream—hallucination—whatever it was, still playing behind my lids, I can't hold them back anymore.

I was right there, living within their heads, feeling their arms—their love. And then it was ripped away within the blink of an eye.

Memories weave with fantasies, choking me along with my tears. I desperately want it to be real, to travel to that time where I was happy and whole.

Whole, like I'll never be again.

The last image flashes across my lids—Alex's twinkling green eyes, bright and full of laughter. His grinning face, overflowing with love. I'd rather remember that false snapshot of him rather than the one that's been stamped in my mind as I was being dragged away. His body bloody, broken beyond repair.

An anguished cry falls softly from my lips before I slap a hand over my mouth. My silence is all that's kept them at bay thus far.

I wish I could fall back into those dreams. I wish I could go back in time. I wish I could return to that made-up memory and never wake. At least I'd be with him again, even if it is in death.

THANK YOU

Thank you so much for reading this Shadows of Synd Novella with Samantha and the Kings!
Continue the series with Running For Shadows.
The Shadows of Synd series is complete and ready for you to enjoy.

If you'd like to hear about the other stories that have been living in my head, sign up for my newsletter (including extra scenes & a novella), visit my website, or follow me on social media visit:
https://emiliaabraham.com

Special Thanks:
K.B. Barrett Designs-Cover Artist and Formatter
Emily Michel-Editor
Emily Renee-Beta Readers

OTHER WORKS

Also by E. Abraham:

Shadows of Synd:
Under the Shadows-Book 1
Between the Shadows-Novella
Running From Shadows-Book 2
Becoming Shadows-Book 3
Shadows Within Us-Book 4
Beyond the Shadows-Book 5

Ruins of Rima: Spin-off Series
Chasing Darkness-Book 1
Charmed by Darkness (December 5, 2023*)*

Available on Newsletter:
Extra Scenes, Bridging Epilogues (Shadows of Synd-Book 1 & 2)

Also by Emilia Abraham:
Stuck at Sundown
Bewitched by Bigfoot: The Cryptid Chronicles

About the Author

After many years of dreaming of becoming a full-time writer, Emilia Abraham took the leap, bringing her words to print. From sweet contemporary romance to spicy why choose and everything in between, she focuses on the happily ever after.

Emilia lives in the Upper Midwest with her husband (who's probably sick of listening to her expound on fictional men) and three kids (who try to steal her post-it notes). When she's not writing, she enjoys reading, playing video games, and consuming copious amounts of energy drinks.